A NOTE TO PARENTS

When your children are ready to "step into reading," giving them the right books is as crucial as giving them the right food to eat. **Step into Reading Books** present exciting stories and information reinforced with lively, colorful illustrations that make learning to read fun, satisfying, and worthwhile. They are priced so that acquiring an entire library of them is affordable. And they are beginning readers with a difference—they're written on five levels.

Early Step into Reading Books are designed for brand-new readers, with large type and only one or two lines of very simple text per page. **Step 1 Books** feature the same easy-to-read type as the Early Step into Reading Books, but with more words per page. **Step 2 Books** are both longer and slightly more difficult, while **Step 3 Books** introduce readers to paragraphs and fully developed plot lines. **Step 4 Books** offer exciting nonfiction for the increasingly independent reader.

The grade levels assigned to the five steps—preschool through kindergarten for the Early Books, preschool through grade 1 for Step 1, grades 1 through 3 for Step 2, grades 2 through 3 for Step 3, and grades 2 through 4 for Step 4—are intended only as guides. Some children move through all five steps very rapidly; others climb the steps over a period of several years. Either way, these books will help your child "step into reading" in style!

Library of Congress Control Number: 2001089028

ISBN: 0-375-81317-9 (trade) — ISBN 0-375-91317-3 (lib. bdg.)

www.randomhouse.com/kids

www.jpinstitute.com

Printed in the United States of America   June 2001   10 9 8 7 6 5 4 3 2

First Edition

STEP INTO READING, RANDOM HOUSE, and the Random House colophon are registered trademarks and the Step into Reading colophon is a trademark of Random House, Inc.

A Note to Parents: This book is appropriate for ages 6 and up. The *Jurassic Park* films are rated PG-13. Consult www.filmratings.com for further information.

Step into Reading®

JURASSIC PARK™

RESCUE MISSION

By Justine and Ron Fontes

A Step 3 Book

Random House 🏠 New York

Chapter 1

The Plan

The last thing Dr. Alan Grant wanted was to return to Jurassic Park. He preferred studying dinosaurs from fossils. *Living* dinosaurs were far too dangerous. He knew that firsthand!

But Grant needed money to continue his studies. And Paul and Amanda Kirby had promised him plenty. All he had to do was point out some dinosaurs as they flew over the island.

Unfortunately, Grant's worst fear soon came true. The plane carrying him, his assistant Billy, the Kirbys, and a pilot had *landed* on the island! They weren't supposed to land!

Everyone got off the plane. Then Amanda began to shout into a bullhorn. *"Eric, are you there, honey?"* Grant wondered who she could be calling.

She got a response that raised the hairs on Grant's neck.

ROARRRRRR!

"Is that a rex?" asked Billy.

Grant shook his head no. "Sounds bigger."

"We gotta go *now*!" said the pilot.

Grant, Billy, and the Kirbys ran back into the plane. The pilot leapt behind the controls. As the plane struggled to take off, it smashed against a giant Spinosaurus and crashed!

The five people were stranded on an island crawling with dinosaurs!

SCRRRIPP! Giant claws tore open the plane as if it was a bag of potato chips. Everyone scrambled out of the wreck.

"This way!" Grant cried, leading the others into the jungle.

ROARRRR!

Billy could not help but look back. The creature was chasing them, crushing small trees with each step! Grant pulled his assistant to safety.

He led the group into a dense grove of
big trees. The huge Spinosaurus could not
squeeze between the thick trunks.

The horrified humans ran until they
thought their lungs would burst. They
were safe . . . for now.

Chapter 2

The Past

Grant turned to Paul Kirby. "Why did you bring us here?"

"Our son is on this island," Amanda Kirby explained. "We need your help to find him."

Paul pulled a photo from his pocket. "Eric is thirteen. He's just about the greatest kid in the world."

Amanda's eyes filled with tears. "We were on vacation. Eric wanted to see the dinosaurs on this island. A friend found a guy who would take him parasailing. But they never came back."

"That was two months ago. We did everything we could, but the U.S. Embassy told us to 'accept the inevitable,'" Paul added.

Grant looked at the pilot. "So you hired this guy to take you here. Then you tricked Billy and me into coming along."

Paul admitted that he and Amanda had lied. He was not a rich man. He was a salesman who had spent his last dime trying to save his son.

"We needed somebody who knew the island," Paul explained.

"You survived the dinosaurs before," Amanda added. "And you saved those other kids."

That was true. But Grant wished he could forget about it. His awful experience in Jurassic Park would haunt him forever.

Oddball billionaire John Hammond had dreamed of a theme park full of living

dinosaurs. Grant had advised against the crazy scheme. But Hammond went ahead with Jurassic Park anyway.

The extinct creatures were created using ancient DNA. Hammond's scientists thought they could control the giant beasts. But nature had proven much stronger than their theories.

Grant had rescued Hammond's grandchildren, and got them off the island safely. He didn't think he could pull off that kind of miracle twice.

In fact, Grant never wanted to see a living dinosaur again. He hoped people had learned a lesson from Jurassic Park. But Grant was not surprised that Hammond's work had lived on. Once people learn *how* to do something, they rarely stop to wonder if they *should*.

Chapter 3

The Present

Grant and the ragged rescuers stopped to catch their breath. They found themselves surrounded by strange craters made of mud and twigs.

Inside the craters were pale eggs the size of potatoes. Grant quickly realized these were nests!

Now the dinosaurs that had been bred in the lab were breeding on their own!

Amanda counted a dozen nests in a neat pattern on the jungle floor.

"Raptors!" Grant gasped.

"What's a raptor?" asked Paul.

Grant looked him in the eye. "If we come across one, we might live," he said.

"Well, that's good," answered Paul.

"But you never come across just *one*,"

Grant replied. Raptors hunted in packs, like lions or wolves. Grant shuddered at the memory of the deadly dinosaurs who had hunted him once before.

Amanda suddenly noticed something. "Where's Billy?" she said. He was gone.

"Billy!" Grant yelled into the thick jungle.

"I thought we weren't supposed to yell," Amanda whispered. Her own cries for Eric had put the Spinosaurus on their trail.

And then suddenly Billy appeared. He came running out of the jungle to Grant. "I got some great pictures of the nests. This proves that raptors raised their young in colonies! We could write a paper!"

Grant sighed. How could Billy think about writing papers at a time like this? Didn't he know that they were in danger?

The Kirbys couldn't forget it for a minute! Their son was somewhere in this jungle. And the Kirbys wanted to find him safe.

At the top of a ridge, the group stopped to catch their breath. They saw a compound of several big buildings in the valley below.

"There's a good chance Eric's in there," Paul said. "I'd bet my bottom dollar."

Grant knew how difficult it was to live on an island with raptors. But he said nothing to discourage the worried parents as they made their way to the deserted compound.

Plants grew up through cracks in the pavement of the parking area. Vine-draped cars and trucks littered the lot like abandoned toys. A horrible stillness hung over the place.

Chapter 4

Inside InGen

Civilization had brought laboratories and lobbies. But the jungle had grown back to reclaim its own.

The windows were all broken, and leaves littered the once-elegant reception desk. Shredded sofas were scattered about the room. Computer screens that had once flickered with the latest software stared blankly beneath a layer of dust.

"Eric! Are you here?" Paul called.

"Eric!" Amanda cried.

But the only answer was the flapping of birds rising from the rafters.

The group entered a huge lab full of equipment for hatching dinosaurs. They saw big tanks full of murky liquid, with pieces of dead dinosaurs floating inside.

Amanda said, "*This* is how they make dinosaurs?"

Grant sighed, disgusted by the sight of science gone mad. "This is how they play God."

The rescuers continued through the deserted lab. Amanda peered into another tank and saw a giant raptor head. She bent down for a closer look. The raptor's eye blinked!

Amanda screamed.

The beast was *behind* the tank, not *in* it! Far from being dead, the raptor lunged at Amanda.

"Back out!" Grant yelled. "Move!"

Luckily, the raptor was too big to fit between the tanks. The humans raced through the lab, seeking a safe haven.

Paul opened the door to a room full of cages. "In here!"

They ran inside with the roaring raptor at their heels. They tricked the raptor into a cage.

"Push!" Amanda cried. She, Grant, and Paul swung the cage door closed, trapping the raptor inside. The cornered creature made a weird, low cry.

Grant was amazed. He had heard that sound before! Billy had used his computer to build a raptor "sound chamber" that made the very same noise. Grant's theory that raptors were social animals was about to be proven correct!

Chapter 5

Raptor Rap

"It's calling for help," said Grant. But this was no time for study.

"Let's go!" Paul cried.

The group raced out of the lab and into the jungle.

The air was filled with weird noises, eerie answers to the trapped raptor's cry. The calls echoed from far and near. The humans were surrounded by raptors, all eager to help one of their own.

"Head for the trees!" Grant yelled.

Then he saw a herd of hadrosaurs. They were running in panic at the sound of the raptors.

Grant led the humans straight into the herd. He hoped the raptors would be distracted by meatier prey.

Suddenly everything was dust and chaos.

But Grant's plan wasn't working. The raptors wove through the herd. They ignored the hadrosaurs. They were tracking the *humans* with deadly determination!

Billy tripped and fell. The strap on his camera bag broke. But the young man was too busy getting back on his feet to notice.

Grant grabbed the fallen bag and looked for its owner. "Billy!" he called.

The student looked back and saw the professor holding his bag. "Alan!" he shouted. But they were soon separated in the confusion.

Grant crashed through thick underbrush. A pack of raptors quickly surrounded him.

The largest female wailed, and the others answered.

Despite the danger, Grant was fascinated by their eerie song. "What does that mean? What are you saying?" He tried to imitate the strange calls. Clearly these creatures were talking about something. But what?

Even as he struggled to understand, Grant realized he may never know.

Chapter 6

Small Survivor

THUD! A can landed at the base of a tree near Grant. A dense fog of oily, smelly smoke poured out of it.

The raptors shrieked in pain. They ran away blindly, tripping over each other in a mad dash to escape the gas.

Grant's eyes watered from the stinging smoke. Through the fog and tears, he could just make out a human figure.

"This way! Hurry!" a voice said.

Grant followed the sound through the fog. A small, dirty hand grabbed his and pulled him along.

As they cleared the circle of smoke, Grant tried to see his rescuer. A cape of leaves was draped over his body, and his head was wrapped in rags. Goggles worn over the rags made the figure even more mysterious. Grant followed blindly through the jungle. He wondered where they were going.

CLANG! A rusty metal door swung shut, leaving them in total darkness. They were inside the stuffy cargo bay of a truck half-sunk in a swamp.

Grant heard fumbling sounds. Then a small, battery-powered lantern flickered dimly. Grant blinked, struggling to see.

The mysterious figure shrugged off his leaf cloak. Then he removed the rags and goggles that hid his filthy face.

The scientist was stunned. His savior was a boy—it had to be *the* boy! But how had he lived for two months on his own?

"Your parents are here," Grant told
Eric.

"On the island?" The boy was amazed. "They'll never make it. I mean, they can't manage when the cable goes out."

Grant thought of the desperate parents who had risked everything for their son. "You'd be surprised what people can do when they have to."

Eric took a closer look at his guest. He knew that face from the jacket of his favorite dinosaur book. "You're Alan Grant. What are *you* doing here?"

"Your parents . . . invited me to come with them . . . to look for you," Grant explained.

"I read both your books. I liked the first one better, before you were on the island. You liked dinosaurs back then," said Eric.

"Back then, they hadn't tried to eat me yet," Grant replied.

The next morning, Grant and Eric left the truck that had been Eric's home for the last two months. They set out to find the others.

Already, Eric was beginning to sound like an excited thirteen-year-old again.

"Know what this is?" he asked Grant.

The scientist took the curved object from the teenager's filthy hand. "A raptor claw. I used to have a fossil of one."

Eric grinned. "Mine's new."

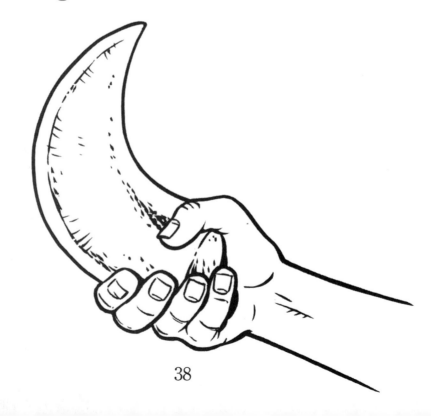

Chapter 7

Reunion

Eric's parents barely recognized their son. But Paul tried to sound upbeat. "I never had a doubt. Never did. Us Kirby men, we stick around, huh?"

Amanda licked her shirttail and tried to clean Eric's grimy face with it.

Paul chuckled. "Honey, there's not enough spit in the world for that."

Amanda laughed for the first time in two months. Her son was safe!

Billy was glad to see Grant, too. "Alan, I'm so sorry. I could have gotten us all killed."

Grant was confused.

"Go ahead and yell at me. Call me an idiot," Billy babbled. Then he asked, "What did you do with them?"

"With what? What are you talking about?" Grant asked.

Billy realized that Grant had no idea what he meant. "Look in my bag," he said.

Grant opened Billy's camera bag. Inside were two raptor eggs.

"I just thought if we could get a raptor back to the mainland, we could study it in a controlled environment," Billy began. "And we could get enough money to fund your research for years!"

Grant was furious. "You're no better than the people who built this place."

Billy had stolen the eggs with no regard for human safety. He had not thought of how the raptors would react.

Suddenly Grant understood why the creatures had followed him instead of chasing the hadrosaurs. They weren't hungry. They were trying to rescue their babies!

The raptors were even smarter than Grant had thought. They had rushed to help one of their own. And they cared deeply for their young.

The raptors had used language *and* teamwork! Getting their eggs back was more important to them than a herd of tasty hadrosaurs.

Grant was eager to get rid of the eggs
that had caused so much trouble. He held
the camera bag over a deep canyon. But
before he could let go, Paul stopped him.

"May I make a suggestion?" the
salesman began. "Keep the eggs with you.
At least until we get off the island." Then

Paul explained, "I'm a parent. If there's one thing I've learned, it's that nothing is more important than your children's safety. And those eggs are the raptors' children. These raptors may want us dead, but they want those eggs more. And that's the only advantage we've got."

Grant realized Paul was right—not just about the eggs, but about families. Maybe dinosaurs weren't so different from people. Both species were moved by their love for their children. Both knew how to work together to accomplish amazing things.

And maybe—just maybe—the humans could trade those precious raptor eggs for safe passage off the island.

And then they could all go home!